SHAWNEE

Big Buddy Books
An Imprint of Abdo Publishing
www.abdopublishing.com

Sarah Tieck

www.abdopublishing.com

Published by Abdo Publishing, a division of ABDO, PO Box 398166, Minneapolis, Minnesota 55439.
Copyright © 2015 by Abdo Consulting Group, Inc. International copyrights reserved in all countries. No part
of this book may be reproduced in any form without written permission from the publisher. Big Buddy Books™
is a trademark and logo of Abdo Publishing.

Printed in the United States of America, North Mankato, Minnesota.
102014
012015

Cover Photo: © NativeStock.com/Angel Wynn; Shutterstock.com.
Interior Photos: © NativeStock.com/Angel Wynn (pp. 5, 9, 13, 16, 17, 21, 23, 25, 26, 27, 29, 30); Shutterstock.com
     (pp. 11, 15, 19).

Coordinating Series Editor: Rochelle Baltzer
Contributing Editors: Megan M. Gunderson, Marcia Zappa
Graphic Design: Adam Craven

Library of Congress Cataloging-in-Publication Data

Tieck, Sarah, 1976-
  Shawnee / Sarah Tieck.
     pages cm. -- (Native Americans)
  Audience: Ages 7-11.
  ISBN 978-1-62403-583-8
  1. Shawnee Indians--Juvenile literature. I. Title.
  E99.S35T54 2015
  974.004'97317--dc23
                              2014030603

CONTENTS

Amazing People

Hundreds of years ago, North America was mostly wild, open land. Native American tribes lived on the land. They had their own languages and **customs**.

The Shawnee (shaw-NEE) are one Native American tribe. They are known for their religious beliefs and powerful fighters. Let's learn more about these Native Americans.

Older Shawnee teach younger people about dances and other traditions.

SHAWNEE TERRITORY

Shawnee homelands were in what is now the central Ohio River Valley. The Shawnee moved as the Iroquois took over their land. Some Shawnee settled in present-day Illinois. Others moved to the southeast or other areas.

CANADA

UNITED STATES

MEXICO

SHAWNEE HOMELANDS

MICHIGAN

PENNSYLVANIA

OHIO

ILLINOIS

INDIANA

WEST VIRGINIA

KENTUCKY

N
W E
S

HOME LIFE

During summer, the Shawnee formed villages. They lived in bark-covered houses. These were built near farm fields. Most villages had a large meeting house. It was used for meetings and religious **ceremonies**.

During winter, the Shawnee moved in search of food. Their winter homes were smaller than their summer homes. They only held one or two people.

Summer homes (*below*) were built to be larger and longer lasting than winter homes.

WHAT THEY ATE

The Shawnee were skilled farmers. They farmed corn, or maize. They also grew beans and pumpkins. Women made maple syrup and gathered wild rice, grapes, nuts, roots, berries, and honey. Men hunted pheasants, deer, bears, and turkeys.

 The Shawnee made animal calls and wore disguises while hunting. This helped them sneak up on prey, such as pheasants.

Daily Life

The Shawnee lived in groups of extended families. They all lived together or close by each other.

The Shawnee wore shirts and moccasins. Women wore skirts. Men wore leggings and **loincloths**. Both men and women had robes to help them stay warm.

Did You Know?

Shawnee children dressed like their parents.

Shawnee villages were often near streams. This made chores, such as washing or fishing, easier.

13

In a Shawnee village, people had different jobs. Men hunted and fished. They used bows, arrows, clubs, and spears. Men also went to war. Both men and women were builders and chiefs.

Shawnee women farmed. They also made crafts, took care of children, and ran the homes. Children learned by helping and watching others in the community.

The Shawnee used bows and arrows (*below*) to kill some of their prey. These weapons were often made from wood and stone.

MADE BY HAND

The Shawnee made many objects by hand. They often used natural materials. These arts and crafts added beauty to everyday life.

Wampum Beads

The Shawnee made shells into wampum beads. They traded them, like money. They also used wampum beads in belt designs. The belts often told stories about people.

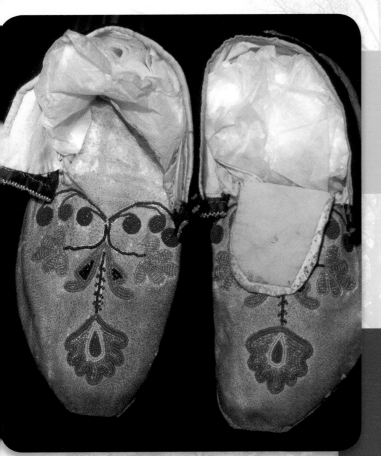

Moccasins

The Shawnee sewed moccasin shoes from animal hides. Some moccasins were decorated with beadwork.

Pottery

Shawnee pottery was formed by hand from clay. It was made to hold things, such as water. Many pieces were considered works of art, too.

Spirit Life

The Shawnee religion focused on a creator goddess called Our Grandmother. The tribe believed she was making a net to sweep up her children on Earth.

The Shawnee held **ceremonies** and **rituals** throughout the year. These focused on nature and seasons. Bread Dances honored the planting and harvesting of crops. The Green Corn Dance took place as crops grew and ripened.

During the Green Corn Dance, the Shawnee gave thanks for their crops.

STORYTELLERS

Stories are important to the Shawnee. The people collect and remember stories to share their **culture** and history. One story tells of how the tribe and the world came to be. This is the Shawnee creation story.

Stories and music are often shared at powwows. At powwows, Native Americans feast, sing, and dance.

FIGHTING FOR LAND

Many people believe the Shawnee are related to early native people known as the Fort Ancient **culture**. This group lived in Ohio between 1000 and 1650. The people were known for building mounds.

In the 1600s, Europeans arrived on Shawnee land. They began to settle there and build colonies. This changed the Shawnee way of life. So, many Shawnee wanted to stop settlement.

The Fort Ancient lived in parts of what is now Ohio, West Virginia, and Kentucky. Today, people have re-created their buildings to learn more about their way of life.

23

In the late 1700s, the Shawnee began to work with other Native American groups. They wanted to stop **colonists** from settling land west of the Appalachian Mountains. They fought many battles. Eventually, colonists moved in.

The Shawnee split into three main groups. These were the Absentee Shawnee, Eastern Shawnee, and Shawnee Tribe.

Over time, many Shawnee settled in Oklahoma. Some were forced to move there. The people used laws to **protect** their way of life and their land.

In 1811, the Shawnee fought in the Battle of Tippecanoe. The Shawnee settlement at Prophetstown was destroyed.

BACK IN TIME

1774

The Shawnee lost an important battle against colonial troops in what is now Point Pleasant, West Virginia.

1670

The Shawnee first met European explorers.

1800s

Chief Tecumseh and his brother Tenskwatawa (*left*) worked to bring together Native Americans west of the Appalachians. This movement ended after they lost the Battle of Tippecanoe in 1811.

1813

Chief Tecumseh died. He had joined with British troops to fight Americans in the War of 1812.

2001

The state of Alabama recognized the Piqua Shawnee as a new branch of Shawnee. Some people do not consider the Piqua a main Shawnee tribe.

1936

Two Shawnee groups became a federally recognized tribe. This means they govern themselves.

THE SHAWNEE TODAY

The Shawnee have a long, rich history. They are remembered for their fierce fighting and skillful farming.

Shawnee roots run deep. Today, the people have kept alive those special things that make them Shawnee. Even though times have changed, many people carry the **traditions**, stories, and memories of the past into the present.

Shawnee wear colorful costumes for dances and events.

"So live your life that the fear of death can never enter your heart. Trouble no one about their religion; respect others in their view, and demand that they respect yours. Love your life, perfect your life, beautify all things in your life. Seek to make your life long and its purpose in the service of your people."

— Chief Tecumseh

GLOSSARY

ceremony a formal event on a special occasion.

colonist a person who lives in a settlement called a colony.

culture (KUHL-chuhr) the arts, beliefs, and ways of life of a group of people.

custom a practice that has been around a long time and is common to a group or a place.

loincloth a simple cloth worn by a man to cover his lower body.

protect (pruh-TEHKT) to guard against harm or danger.

ritual (RIH-chuh-wuhl) a formal act or set of acts that is repeated.

tradition (truh-DIH-shuhn) a belief, a custom, or a story handed down from older people to younger people.

WEBSITES

To learn more about Native Americans, visit **booklinks.abdopublishing.com**. These links are routinely monitored and updated to provide the most current information available.

31

INDEX